Dandelions, Fireflies, and Rhubarb Pie

Dandelions, Fireflies, and Rhubarb Pie

*The Adventures of Grandma Bagley
and Her Friends*

by

Ethel Marbach

Illustrated by William Myers

The Upper Room

Nashville, Tennessee

Dandelions, Fireflies, and Rhubarb Pie

Book Design: Harriette Bateman
First Printing: June, 1984 (10)
Library of Congress Catalog Card Number: 84-51403
ISBN: 0-8358-0481-X
Printed in the United States of America

Contents

Introduction

When we plant a tiny seed in the earth, it is with the hope that in time a flower will grow. We know from past experience that rain and sunshine will help the plant to grow. So we wait until at last through the dirt comes one tiny green shoot. It is a promise of what is to come. Then begins the longer process of waiting until the leaves grow, the plant gets taller and finally buds appear. Waiting just a little longer, with care, a little more sunshine and water, a little bit of color begins to come to these green buds. At long last, we discover the bud has opened to a beautiful yellow flower. Our happiness is complete, because we have planted, cared for, watched over, and now can celebrate the brightness of the flower.

This book has been like a tiny seed, first the dream of one person, and was shared with other people, who helped develop the ideas. There was a period of waiting and planning. Contact was made with Mary Lu Walker, the songwriter and singer for the cassette. She had lots of ideas about the project. She wrote new songs. Then Ethel Marbach was contacted and asked if she would write some new stories. She also had lots of ideas of the kinds of stories that were needed. Gene Cotton, a musician, was contacted and asked if he would help with the recording process. He said that he would be glad to help.

There were meetings held in several different cities of these interested people. And finally the project began to grow. *Pockets* magazine was contacted and asked if they would like to publish the stories. When the stories appeared in *Pockets,* beautiful illustrations were added. Upper Room Press accepted the idea of publishing this book and cassette that you have now.

Then came the day when Mary Lu Walker, Gene Cotton, and the musicians came to Nashville to record the songs. It was done in a famous recording studio. Gene Cotton worked his magic and Mary Lu sang her best, and soon the cassette tape was finished. All the while that this was going on, the staff of the Upper Room were working on the book. Until finally "the flower," *Dandelions, Fireflies, and Rhubarb Pie* was ready for you.

This project has been funded through money contributed by individuals in congregations of the United Methodist Church.* May you enjoy it and learn to love both the stories and the songs.

Team Members:
    Richard L. Cookson, Project Team Chairperson
MaryJane Pierce Norton, Janice Grana, Judy Smith, Mary Lu Walker, Ethel Marbach, and Gene Cotton.

    *A joint project of the General Board of Discipleship and the Upper Room.

* 1 *

Around the Kitchen Table

It was a blustery, snowy January afternoon when Grandma Bagley wiped the flour dust from her hands onto her apron and hurried to open the back door. She had seen her friends coming, four of them this time, counting the dog. They looked like finger puppets, their bright caps bobbing up and down as they made a path to the door.

"Come in, come in, my goodness," she whisked them through the door, even the snow-frosted beast of a dog. "Don't let the heat out! Quickly, into the kitchen, and stand on the rug, if you please!"

The children stood quietly in a small dripping clump, saying nothing. Grandma Bagley stood with her hands on her hips and said, "Well, what do we have today? Three red-nosed snowpeople and one Abominable Snowdog with swishing tail! Come on, give me your jackets and we'll get them dry." She hung them on pegs behind the big black stove, where they dripped onto newspapers on the floor. Moose, for that was the dog's name, shook himself violently, flinging snow to all corners of the kitchen, and then lay down under the table, stretching in grateful content.

The children huddled around the stove as if it were a summer bonfire and they were toasting marshmallows. They wiped their noses with the tissues Grandma Bagley offered, their eyes quietly hypnotized by the large yellow mounds covering the table like oversized polkadots on a dress. They were lemon sugar cookies, and it was their heavenly smell that had turned them from the sidewalk to Grandma Bagley's path without a moment's hesitation.

"Anthony, I see you've brought Jenny Rose today," said Grandma Bagley to break the silence. Anthony pretended not to hear. He looked out the window and scratched his head. Jenny Rose, who was Anthony's little sister, ran over to Grandma Bagley and grabbed her by the leg.

"I'd like a cookie, please, please, *please. . . .*"

"Good heavens," gasped Grandma Bagley, "if I value my leg, I'd better give you one at once." And she popped one in Jenny Rose's mouth and told the others to help themselves.

"Go on, all of you, and let me see you smile for goodness sake! Such a glum bunch you are today! No stories, nothing to share? I think you've got a case of the winter glumps. Things get that way after Christmas, you know. You feel all glumpy and fizzled, as if the air's been let out of your balloon. And you get bored with snow and losing mittens and getting your boot zippers stuck. Oh, I know how it is. And then everything that bothers you seems twice as bad."

Grandma Bagley knew about most of the things that bothered them. Margaret Mary, better known as Maggie, was shy as a deer and felt lost when she had to leave her house. She was part of a large family, right smack in the middle of three older sisters and three younger brothers—and, of course, Moose, the dog. When she was with them, she felt warm and secure, because she knew they loved her and didn't even notice her eyes. Outside of the family, it was different. Maggie wore big round glasses over her brown eyes which were very weak and slightly crossed. Most of the time she looked down at her feet when she talked to people, so they would not stare at her.

Anthony seemed to have a different problem each time he came. Most of his problems were due to his annoyance at having to do things he didn't want to do!

"What is it this time, Big Chief Thunder Cloud?" asked Grandma Bagley, offering another cookie.

"Oh, it's just that I had to take care of *her* today," he grumbled, pointing at Jenny Rose, "—thank you—I had this very important basketball practice and they *needed* me. And then I had to drag *her* along after school because my mom and dad have to work late, and she won't just sit still and watch. She runs after the ball and the fellas trip over her. She's just one big pest!"

Jenny Rose was not listening. She was flat on her stomach, trying to reach Max, the black-and-white cat, curled up under the stove. Grandma Bagley kept her smiles inside and turned to Maggie. "And what about you, Princess Rain-in-the-Face?" Maggie looked down at her feet and then at Jenny Rose and then at the spider plant hanging in the window. She told Grandma Bagley that today in gym she was the only one left when they picked teams for volleyball. No one wanted her, so they put her name on a piece of paper, and the captains closed their eyes and picked, and everyone on the team she got on groaned and rolled their eyes when she walked over.

Poor dear, Grandma Bagley thought, but she said nothing. Instead she smiled and said, "Enough of this gloom and doom. I never heard such glumpering and wivvering and snidling in all my life!"

Grandma Bagley set out a big earthenware bowl and some mixing spoons. "Do you ever think that other people have problems just like you, even mean people? Nothing and nobody in this world is perfect. Some people are born blind or crippled or have fluttery hearts or slow brains. *All* of us are born into lives we didn't choose—your father might be a professor in Sweden or a plumber in Portugal, or you might have red hair or black skin.

"Would you believe that when I was a little girl, I would have given anything for long, dark, straight hair I could braid, instead of short red curly hair? I hated it. When it rained, I looked as if I were plugged into a socket, it frizzed up so. And at night, I would cry myself to sleep because I had to wear brown cotton stockings held up with a piece of elastic, instead of the white silk ones with blue garters the other girls had, and because I had to bring my lunch in a paper sack, and sometimes it was just last night's cold baked potato. This might not seem much to you, but it hurt so much then, I can still remember how I felt. So we all

13

have things that can hurt us if we let them. It's up to us to decide if we'll spend our lives feeling sorry for ourselves. *Now. . . .*"

As she talked, Grandma Bagley bustled and busied and moved this and that. She didn't like to waste time doing just one thing. "How would you like to make"—and she stopped dramatically until she had every child's attention—"a Three Kings Cake? Today is Epiphany, the day the Three Kings found the baby Jesus, so let's celebrate! Unless you'd rather sulk and think what a terrible life you have! Anthony, you're dropping crumbs all over Maggie's feet." Anthony giggled, "That's all right, Moose is licking them off."

"We shall now make an incredibly delicious concoction called Eggless, Milkless, Butterless Cake, which my dear grandmother used to make during World War I, when they didn't have any of those things. And each of you will have a cake to take home with you."

"If there's nothing in it, how can you make a cake?" asked Maggie, looking directly at Grandma Bagley.

"I didn't say *nothing*. I said no eggs or milk or butter. You see, in those days, everything was in short supply, so we just had to use our imagination and wits to make something delicious out of what we *did* have, instead of fussing about what we didn't. A bit like my accepting my red hair and looking for something good about it. For one thing, I always stood out in a crowd! Anthony, you get the flour and cinnamon and nutmeg and cloves and then please grease these three pans. Maggie, measure the sugar and raisins and oil into the water and watch it till it boils. Anthony, you beat everything together till it's brown and satiny. Yes, yes, Jenny Rose, you may lick the spoon. And everyone gets the bowl."

Grandma Bagley stepped away from the table, which seemed like a windmill of activity going at full tilt. There was a hum and clatter of squeals and dropped spoons and spice cans and flour and raisins on the floor. She closed her eyes and thanked Heaven that Moose was such a good vacuum cleaner.

"Very good, my dears, and now we add the finishing touch." She took a blue willowware teapot from the cabinet, reached in, and brought out a handful of change. She gave each child a penny, nickel, and dime. Now drop them into the batter," she ordered. "Go ahead, Maggie, it won't hurt the cake."

"I never heard of putting money in a cake," said Maggie.

"It's to honor the Three Kings, who each brought his own special gift to the Christ child," said Grandma Bagley. "Whoever gets the dime is King or Queen for a day, and you can do anything you want."

"*Anything?*" they all asked at once.

"Anything!"

"Can I fly to England on a bathmat?"

"Absolutely."

"Can I eat 722 M&Ms and not get sick?"

"It is possible."

"Can I get my eyes uncrossed?" asked Maggie.

"Can I *lose* a sister?" muttered Anthony, but softly so Jenny Rose would not hear.

"My dears," sighed Grandma Bagley, "I am not

the Wizard of Oz and I can't grant today's desires of your hearts. But tomorrow you will want something different and you will wonder why today's wishes were so important. In the meantime, each of you has a lovely cake which you can share with your family right *now*."

And she took the cakes out of the oven, all brown and puffed up with raisins bursting through the top crust. "Heavenly," exclaimed Grandma Bagley, breathing deeply. "Heavenly as always."

On top of each of the cakes, she poured a circle of white icing and onto this set a crown of red and green and orange and purple gumdrops. The children zipped up their jackets, pulled on their boots, and pulled down their caps. Grandma Bagley wrapped the cakes in waxed paper and gave Moose one last lemon cookie and a shriveled frankfurter she found in the refrigerator.

"Now, straight home with you, and don't nibble or poke around to find the dime. You've got to do this fair and square. If anyone cheats, Moose will turn into a porcupine right on the spot. Jenny Rose, *don't* poke. . . ."

Anthony groaned, "If she gets the dime, I'll just *die*."

Maggie laughed happily and threw her head back, and her fat sausage pigtails bobbed and danced. She didn't say so out loud, but she thought Grandma Bagley must have been wrong when she said nothing was ever perfect. She held the Three Kings Cake up to her nose and smelled the warm fragrance and thought it the most perfect thing in the world.

Grandma Bagley's
Heavenly Eggless, Milkless, Butterless Cake

Boil together for 3 minutes **1 cup dark brown sugar,
1½ cups water, ⅓ cup oil, 2 cups raisins (dark), 2
tsp. cinnamon, ½ tsp. cloves, ½ tsp. nutmeg.** Cool.
Then add **1 tsp. baking soda** mixed in **2 tsp. water.**
Blend in **2 cups flour** and **1 tsp. baking powder.**
Pour into a greased round tube pan (or several little
pans), and bake in a 325-degree oven for about 50 minutes (or 20 minutes for smaller cakes). Turn onto a
rack and let cool. Ice with plain vanilla icing. Make a
crown of gumdrops or M&Ms in center of cake for
Three Kings Cake. Add nuts if you like. Or bake in an
8-inch pan and serve plain with confectioners' sugar
sprinkled on top.

* 2 *

Mrs. Lucas's Mittens

Grandma Bagley was ready and waiting at the kitchen door when Kate and her mother drove up. Thursday was her Going-out-to-Eat-Supper day, and she prepared for it as carefully as if she were having tea with the Queen Mother. She wore her white gloves and pearl necklace and Lily-of-the-Valley perfume and brushed her white hair into a puff which looked like a dandelion gone to seed. She looked forward to her Thursday evenings because she enjoyed eating other people's cooking, and it also gave her a chance to cheer up her friends who had a tendency to be glum.

Kate looked forward to Thursdays, too. For her, it was as exciting as going to the library. She had no brothers or sisters or pets, and sometimes she felt so lonely that she wished she could live in a large, noisy family like Maggie's and have a large, sloppy dog like Moose. Kate spent most of her time in the library, making friends with the fairies and animals and people she found inside the books. But on Thursdays, she shut her books, climbed into the car beside her mother, and carefully held trays of good-smelling food which she and her mother picked up after letting Grandma Bagley off at the Senior Citizens Center.

Kate liked the way older people listened to her tales of the week's happenings and the way their eyes crinkled when they smiled and how they smelled of lilac talcum powder when they bent over to thank her. She liked the way Mr. Muggeridge dropped cigar ashes on his vest and didn't bother to brush them off when he pulled out his gold watch from his pocket. And she liked the way Mrs. White (who was black) always offered her butter mints from a pink glass dish.

The one person she did not really like to visit was Mrs. Lucas, because her house smelled of unpleasant things—things gone bad or stale or sour. Mostly, though, it smelled of cats. Mrs. Lucas had eight cats— all sizes and colors and dispositions. And many of them were mothers, with little batches of kittens tucked away here and there. Kate learned quickly not to sit down without checking for furry creatures underneath. They slept wherever they pleased—on the kitchen table, the fireplace mantel, or the top of the refrigerator where they stared at Kate with serious dislike.

Mrs. Lucas often forgot to put away opened cans of cat food or cartons of milk. Dirty clothes lay in little piles on dusty, sticky floors. Bags of garbage huddled in a bunch in dark corners. Half-cups of tea sat everywhere, with the green mold growing on top undisturbed.

But Mrs. Lucas herself was nice. Even though her hair was often uncombed and the front of her dress soiled from the food she had spilled, and wrinkled stockings hung on her swollen legs, she was always sweet and gracious. When she heard Kate's knock, she answered with a gentle, "Come in, my dear, the door's open." When Kate would say, "Hello, Mrs. Lucas, it's Kate," the old woman would smile, "Why Kate, what a sweet child you are to bring me all these goodies! Now what do we have tonight?"

And Kate would peel the aluminum foil off the plastic plate, set it on Mrs. Lucas's small tin E.T. tray with the folding legs, and tell her. Sometimes it would be a piece of ham with sweet potato, sometimes creamed chicken on biscuit. Kate would always wait until Mrs. Lucas would shakily put the fork to her lips to be sure she could manage it, for Mrs. Lucas was almost completely blind.

"I don't know how she survives," Kate's mother would say. "She would really be better off in a nursing home." But Mrs. Lucas would not leave the cottage which had been her home for over fifty years. She had come here as a bride and here she would stay, and she would not give in to sadness. She knew she must fill her days with work which she could do and which would give her satisfaction. So Mrs. Lucas knitted mittens.

Since she could not see the colors distinctly—she could barely make out the darks from the lights—she did not bother with patterns or design. She tied bits and pieces of yarn together and just kept on knitting. She had once made mittens which sold at fairs and which people clamored to buy—mittens with designs of snowmen and hearts and fir trees. She could no longer do this, so she blended everything together—like a huge pot of soup—and the scarlets and blues and lime greens and oranges came together like a small miracle to make mittens of unique beauty. No two alike, except by chance.

When she ran out of yarn, she began unraveling sweaters and afghans. Soon she had piles of mittens growing up from the floor, stacked on the couch between sleeping cats, under her bed, in the refrigerator. Still, she kept on knitting, because if she stopped, she would have nothing to do.

This Thursday, Kate brought Mrs. Lucas her dinner of creamed chipped beef, baked potato, and green beans. Kate did not usually look around, but for some reason today the room had a gay look. Kate noticed, for the first time, the stacks of bright patches growing higher at Mrs. Lucas's feet.

"Oh," she said out loud, "what *beautiful* mittens! I've never seen anything like them—why, there are no two alike! There must be hundreds of them—oh, look at that one!" and she pulled out a blue-and-white striped mitten with a pink thumb.

"Do you like them?" asked Mrs. Lucas, with quiet pleasure. "Please take another, my dear, and make a pair. I don't know what they look like. Not very pretty, I'm afraid, but these old eyes can't do much better. If you poke around, you might find one to match."

And Kate did! She could not believe her good fortune. Wait till she showed her friends at school!

Kate's mother said nothing when Kate bounced back into the car wearing her new mittens with pink thumbs. All the way home, Kate talked of nothing but her gift from Mrs. Lucas. Well, thought Kate's mother, it was almost the end of winter, and Kate would probably lose them as she did all her mittens, and that would be the end of that.

At school the next day, Kate's friends crowded around her to see and feel and try on her new mittens, and she told them the story of how she had gotten them.

"Does she really have any more?" asked Peter.

"Piles of them," said Kate.

"And would she really give them away?" insisted Peter.

"Why don't you ask her yourself?"

"All right, I will! Will you show us where she lives?"

That afternoon, Kate took Peter and Maggie and Anthony and Timothy to meet Mrs. Lucas. "I brought some of my friends, Mrs. Lucas. They like your mittens."

Mrs. Lucas was overjoyed. "Well, I'm so glad—how many of you are there, children?" She squinted, trying to make out the blurs which kept moving.

"There are five of us, Mrs. Lucas, and my name is Peter."

Then, as the others introduced themselves by name, Mrs. Lucas invited each to take a pair of mittens. And so they did, with soft squeals and giggles as they dug through the piles for just the right ones. Timothy, who chose a pair with green and white polka dots and orange thumbs, asked if Mrs. Lucas needed anything from the store.

"Well, now that you mention it—I could use a bag

of cat food, a box of arrowroot cookies, and a can of peppermint tea. Thank you so much, Timothy."

Timothy could not wait to tell his family and neighbors about Mrs. Lucas, because she had long been a mystery to them. They had wondered about the lady who lived in the cottage that seemed left over from another time.

The next afternoon, Timothy returned with his friends Loretta and Moxie and Leonard and Sulamith. They came in a bit timidly, but soon they were laughing and eating vanilla wafers and trying to pet the cats who were hiding under the couch. They looked in secret glances about the house which had been such a mystery to them and were disappointed with its shabbiness. They saw all the things that needed to be fixed and cleaned, but they did not know how to ask if they could help.

"Please don't leave without taking a pair of mittens. Go on, any pair you want!" Mrs. Lucas said. They scrambled quickly and got in each other's way, but did not argue over their choices. Each mitten was as beautiful as the other. Moxie held up her mittened hands in wide-eyed delight.

"Look, it's like wearing a rainbow!" she cried, and in her excitement, she stepped on Mrs. Lucas's foot and gave her a tight hug.

"Can we come and do something for you sometime?" asked Leonard.

"Oh no, that's not necessary. . . . Well, now that you mention it—these windows—they're nailed shut for winter, and now that it's getting warmer, I would like to get a breath of fresh air."

The next afternoon, Timothy and his friends from the neighborhood, and Kate and all Timothy's other friends from school, came and began the job of trying to put the cottage into shape. They almost didn't know where to begin. First, they washed the windows, inside and out. Then they pulled out the nails and opened the windows and put up a few screens they found in Mrs. Lucas's shed. They scrubbed the kitchen and bathroom floors and tied up bags of trash and put them out by the curb.

They swept cobwebs from the ceiling with a broom and shook mountains of dust from rag rugs outside. They washed dirty dishes and scoured the sink and put away the plastic bags of cookies Mrs. Lucas had left on the stove burners and forgotten about. They hung up her nightie and shook crumbs from her sheets and mopped up the colony of dust bunnies under her bed. Mrs. Lucas, with tears in her eyes and the bedroom slippers found under her bed now on her feet, gave them each another pair of mittens to give to a friend.

Soon, all their mothers and fathers and teachers knew about Mrs. Lucas and wanted to help her, too. Their class held a rummage sale and raised $10.65 to buy her new yarn of every color imaginable (they used 65¢ to buy a card on which they all signed their names). Every week, Maggie's mother made her pots of vegetable soup or clam chowder. Peter's mother, who worked in a beauty parlor, came and washed and brushed Mrs. Lucas's wisps of white hair into a halo around her face.

Anthony's father, who owned a fruit and vegetable

market, brought her strawberries and fresh spinach and potatoes. Timothy's mother came and helped her roll the yarn into balls and listened to her stories of when she was a young teacher. Kate's mother bought rolls of bright, white wallpaper with forget-me-nots on it, which Kate's father and Peter and Anthony helped put up. It was good that Mrs. Lucas couldn't see too clearly, because Peter and Anthony put a few strips on upside down.

And still, Mrs. Lucas kept knitting. There were no longer piles of mittens on the floor or under the bed or in the refrigerator, for as fast as she would knit a pair, someone would appear who needed them. And that person would always turn out to be a new friend who would ask, "Is there anything I can do for you, Mrs. Lucas?"

One evening, Mrs. Lucas finished a pair of black-and-white checked mittens with glittery red thumbs and set them on the kitchen table for tomorrow's visitor, whoever it might be. She made her way carefully across the floor littered with sleeping cats. She took off her clothes and dropped them in a little pile onto the floor where she could find them easily in the morning. She put on her fresh, clean nightie and lay down be-

tween the fresh clean sheets. Her heart was so grateful, she knew she could not squeeze in one more drop of contentment. She had been so blessed with new friends. How could she ever repay them for their kindness? She fell asleep asking God to help her find just the right way.

And Kate, before going to bed this same evening, laid her blue-and-white striped mittens with the pink thumbs in a special, secret box, which already held a dead Monarch butterfly she had found on the road, a deep blue feather from a jay, a white stone shaped like a heart, a bookmark with a pressed dried shamrock. She added them to her dearest treasures so they would never get lost.

* 3 *

Maggie's Mother
and the Goose

Grandma Bagley had been transplanting seedlings all day, and she was weary. She had begun right after breakfast separating the tender sprouts and had worked right through lunch until the very moment Maggie arrived from school. The kitchen table was covered with paper cups and tin cans and egg shells with plants eager to grow on their own. A disappointed Maggie had hoped to find cookies there instead.

Grandma hugged her, dirty hands and all, and then sat down on a stool with a thump and a sigh. "I am *so* glad to see you, Maggie. I'm right on the verge of getting grumpy. All this work and no play makes one grumpy and dull—and hungry. Let's see what we can dig up. . . . Hummm—how about graham crackers and peanut butter? Suitable, I'd say, but not exciting."

She muttered as she spread the crackers, "I do this every year. When will I ever learn? I plant too many seeds, get too many plants, can't bear to throw one away. . . ."

She was interrupted by a wheezing, screeching chugging coming up the driveway. It was a sound both of them knew and welcomed—the Saybrook Farm milk truck. Grandma jumped up. "Oh, good! It's Joe, just in time for milk with our crackers. Dear Joe, he always comes at the right moment!"

That's exactly what Maggie's mother said when Joe drove up into *their* driveway. It was always the right moment whenever he came, for he was a special friend who brought more than milk and yogurt into their lives. At first he frightened Maggie a bit because he was so tall and had bushy eyebrows that hung like awnings over his crinkly eyes. When he laughed, it was a booming Santa Claus HO HO HO that wobbled the pictures on the wall. But she soon discovered that his heart was as large as his voice, not only for her family, but also for everyone on his route.

For one thing, he collected some people's discards and passed them on to others who could use them. Maggie's mother called him God's Tinker and explained to Maggie that a tinker was a peddler or gypsy who sold things like pots and pans and pencils door to door. But Maggie knew Joe was a giver, not a seller. He would give her a carton of chocolate milk, to keep her strength up he said, and then he would produce a surprise for her mother—a braided rug, wind chimes, day-old doughnuts, grapevine cuttings. And always, Maggie's mother would throw up her hands and say that was exactly what she had wished for!

Today, Joe gave Grandma Bagley a magnificent

bunch of fresh rhubarb which helped her weariness disappear. "Now I'll *know* it's spring," she exclaimed, "when I get that first pie in the oven and it runs over and I smell that syrup burning! Now, Joe, will you take these oodles of plants and distribute them along the way? You, too, Maggie. Here's a carton of pepper plants for your mother. Just plant them in their egg shells; they're all ready to go."

"Okay, come on, Maggie, you can ride home with me," boomed Joe. "I've got something special for your mother, too." Maggie threw a kiss to Grandma and climbed into the old truck, which her mother said must be held together with toothpicks, chewing gum, and prayer. She sat in the cool dark back, drinking her

chocolate milk carefully so it wouldn't spill as they rumbled over the bumps.

As the truck shivered to a halt at Maggie's house, Maggie saw her mother digging in the garden, feeding the soil with coffee grounds and small dead fish her brothers had found on the lakeshore. Maggie jumped out and ran towards her with her egg carton gift. Joe followed, carrying a large brown sack and booming, "Anybody home?"

Maggie's mother stood up, glad for a break from digging, and smiled over the gift of plants. "Peppers—great! We can always squeeze them in somewhere."

Then Joe handed her the brown sack and stood back, beaming expectantly, as if he had just given her the treasure of the universe. Maggie's mother opened it and gasped. She reached in and slowly, gingerly, pulled out a large white goose, quite dead.

"How about this goose, Mrs. McCarthy? Poor old fella walked right into my truck, just like that! The lady who owned him said it was sad but it's his own fault for being so dumb. If he had any brains, he wouldn't be dead, now, would he? This will make you one good meal—you ever have roast goose, Maggie?" Maggie shook her head and looked down at her feet. Her glasses were getting blurry from the tears which were slowly escaping, one by one.

"Why, you know, that's the best-tasting—Say, it's better than chicken or turkey anyday. Just ask your mommy."

Maggie's mother smiled slowly and said, "Thanks, Joe. It's really nice of you to think of us, but I've never eaten goose either."

"Oh, that's no problem. You just cook it like you would a chicken. After you clean out the insides. And after you pluck the feathers. . . . I don't think that'll be hard, he's still warm. And then you'll have all these nice soft feathers for a pillow, Maggie. . . ."

Maggie's mother nodded and thanked Joe for his kindness. Then he waved good-bye, climbed into his truck, and was off to his next customer. Maggie's mother returned to her digging. *If only*, she thought, *I had been brought up on a farm and was used to killing chickens and pigs and lambs for food. But I wasn't, and I hate the thought of killing anything whose eyes I can look into. Still, this is a gift, and I didn't kill it, and shouldn't waste it.* She had no choice. She must pluck the goose feathers quickly and get it over with.

She sent Maggie up to the bedroom for a clean pillow case and started tugging at the feathers, but they wouldn't come. She tried another spot, and then another, getting only a small handful of white fluff which went through her fingers and up into the air. The goose flopped up and down with each tug and its eye seemed to look accusingly at Maggie's mother. Wearily, she stopped.

"I give up. Sorry, Maggie, I don't have the heart for it. I feel as if I am an animal tearing my brother apart. And if I can't pluck it, we can't eat it, so that's the end of that."

"That's okay, Mom," said Maggie, relieved. "I don't think I could've eaten it anyway."

Now, they wondered, what should they do with it? The garden was already planted, so they couldn't bury him there. "I think I know where he should go," said her mother. "Get Kevin and Danny and Martin and they can carry him over to the dump behind the cemetery. At least he'll be out of the way." *Out of sight and out of mind,* she thought.

Kevin and Danny and Martin, who were Maggie's brothers, carried the goose across the street, through the cemetery, to the dump scattered with old Christmas wreaths and plastic daffodils and faded satin ribbons. They laid him on top of a spray of red and yellow gladiolas turning brown and took their time coming back, kicking pebbles along the road and playing leapfrog over the tombstones. In the daytime, the cemetery was a pleasant extension of their back-yard where they came to play and leave small bunches of dandelions on graves with no flowers.

Supper was already waiting for them when they got back—clam chowder with biscuits three inches high, and apple crisp for dessert. Their father, who was a doctor at the hospital, was working late, so they began without him.

Maggie's mother was very quiet during the meal. She didn't seem to notice that Kevin and Danny and Martin were eating with dirty hands, and that Sheila and Jane were kicking each other under the table. Maggie was also quiet and ate her soup slowly, making sure all the clams were left in a huddle at the bottom of the bowl.

Finally, Maggie's mother spoke. "Children, stop your bickering and listen to me. I think I did something wrong today and now I'm sorry for it. I sent you boys over to dump that goose in the cemetery, and now

I think of him lying there, on top of all that garbage, exposed to the crows and hawks and rats and foxes," she shuddered. "He was such a beautiful bird, and I don't think it was right for me to throw him into the garbage as if he were a rotten cabbage or empty oatmeal box."

The children looked at her blankly, not knowing what to expect. If she didn't want to throw him out or eat him, what would she do with him? *Maybe she wanted to stuff him,* thought Sheila, *and keep him in the living room by the pot of geraniums.*

"I think we should go over to the cemetery and bring him back," said Maggie's mother. Everyone was silent. Twilight was settling into a deep evening purple. They were not sure of the cemetery by night. "I'll go with you," she said. "If we go right now, we can still have light to see." With their mother joining them, their bravery returned.

They set off at a brisk walk, laughing and shivering, watching the tall pine trees turn black against the sky. The tombstones seemed to be unfriendly, frowning granite chess pieces. By the time they reached the back of the cemetery, the dump was already dark. They heard the rustle and scratching of small animal feet skittering over cans and baskets. The rats had arrived early, smelling perhaps a special feast. A little wind stirred the quivering aspens to high, fluttery sighs. Kevin found the white spot which was the goose, picked his way through the wreaths and old flowers, grabbed the goose, flung it over his shoulder and began to run. Then all of them, seized with a sudden, unnamed fear, started to run, blindly, in all directions. From a clump of dark pines came the sound of a plaintive whining cry, repeated over and over.

Maggie began to cry and squeezed her mother's hand as they ran.

"What's that?" she sniffled.

"Just a whippoorwill, honey," said her mother.

"Whimperwill?"

"That's right, Wimper Will—he's a big crybaby," her mother laughed.

The little girls squealed.

"I saw eyes behind that tombstone, big green eyes. It's a ghost and he's going to get us!" wailed Jane.

The goose flopped faster and harder against Kevin's back, as he leaped over the tombstones. The other boys followed, and their shadows, in the light of the half moon, danced in and out of the graves. Finally, they reached the street, and then the safety of their home. They flung themselves on the grass, their cheeks blazing and hearts fluttering. Maggie's mother, a bit out of breath herself, covered the goose with an old blanket and said, "I think we need something, like dessert." And they all went in for bowls of apple crisp with vanilla ice cream.

The next morning, Maggie's mother and father buried the goose in the earth beneath the wild blackberry bramble, where he would lie at peace and undisturbed. When Joe came the next day and asked how they had enjoyed their meal of roast goose, Maggie's mother told him what had happened, and he laughed and slapped his knee and shook his head as if it were the greatest joke he ever heard.

"I'm sorry, Joe," said Maggie's mother, "but I guess I'd rather eat turnips the rest of my life than pluck a goose. But your gift will nourish us anyway—I planted him under the blackberry bush!"

And she was right. The following year, their blackberry buckets overflowed with berries as thick as your thumb. Maggie's mother made hundreds of blackberry pies and hundreds of jars of blackberry jelly, or so it seemed to Maggie. And, of course, it was all because of the goose.

4

Off with Their Heads!

Peter enjoyed cutting Grandma Bagley's lawn as much as she enjoyed having him do it. It was, she told him, "a mutually beneficial arrangement." When he asked what that meant, she told him that they each helped each other. She liked to sit on her porch and see a neat, well-trimmed lawn. An uncut lawn reminded her of a fellow who needed a haircut, she said, and it made her itch. And Peter needed money to go to basketball camp this summer. His mother, who worked long hours as a hairdresser to support them, was able to pay half the cost; but Peter would have to earn the rest. And that is why cutting Grandma Bagley's lawn was mutually beneficial. But it was more than a job for Peter. He ran all the way from school in his zest to get that lawn mower out of the shed and get to work. It was the old-fashioned push kind, with no cord or motor, nothing but sharp, shearing blades obeying completely the whim of its master. Peter was no longer Peter in torn, grass-stained sneakers and patched jeans. He became the Head Cheese, the Commander-in-Chief, the King to whom everyone bowed. He ruled sternly and sometimes mercilessly as he pushed the

mower up and down, back and forth, around the rose-bushes and the horse chestnut tree and the old well, allowing no flaw to mar his perfect country.

Peter loved the sight of grass flying up from the blades in a green spray, with the heads of clover and daisies and dandelions mixed in. Dandelions especially! No matter how hard he tried to destroy them, a few would pop up to tease him. As if they didn't know he could wipe them out in a flash! They annoyed him as much as the ants who had the nerve to build their mound home in the center of the lawn.

He didn't like bugs any more than dandelions. He didn't lop off *their* heads with the lawn mower, but he would step on beetles, June bugs, ants—anything that crawled. Except spiders. Spiders he left alone. He used to pick them off the windows he washed for Grandma in spring and flush them down the sink, and in one wipe ruin their evening's work of weaving webs. Sometimes, he would suck up both web and spider with the vacuum cleaner. Once, after doing this, he had a nightmare of a huge, black spider, growing larger and larger within the vacuum cleaner bag, until finally it broke through the machine and began climbing the stairs to his room on its eight hairy legs, muttering with glee, "Peter, Peter, Spider-killer, I'm going to get you, wait and see!" He never vacuumed another spider.

Peter was not a cruel boy. He did not tear the wings off flies or butterflies just to be mean. But he was thoughtless. He did not think of birds or cats or chipmunks as part of the family of God. He had once killed a bird, but not on purpose. He had skimmed a rock at two birds sitting still as clothespins on a telephone wire. He wanted to see them scatter and fly off twittering. But the rock found its mark, and one bird fell to the ground, straight down without a flutter.

Peter's heart had seemed to freeze. He knew the bird must be dead. He picked up the still-warm body and said, "I'm sorry, I'm sorry; I didn't mean it." Then he hid it under a pile of leaves by a honeysuckle bush. Nobody had seen him except God, and God knew it was an accident. But if he had not thrown the rock. . . . He had forgotten about that bird until today.

Just then Grandma came out to compliment Peter on his good work and to remind him to trim the edges. He put on a performance for her, angrily mowing down a patch of dandelions that had escaped execution.

"My goodness, Peter, don't get so riled up!" she said. "You remind me of the Red Queen in *Alice in Wonderland.* Remember? She kept shouting, 'Off with their heads!' every time someone annoyed her. What have you got against those poor dandelions?"

"They're just weeds and they don't belong here. They're a bother. I cut them down and they just come back. You'd think that they would know better and that I'm going to get them with the lawn mower anyhow!"

"Why, Peter, they've got just as much right to grow as you do. God put them here, yes, right here on my lawn. They can't help their nature or where they were planted any more than you can. Myself, I just love dandelions. They are such rascals. Did you ever notice they seem to bloom best where no one wants them?"

"Yes!" exploded Peter.

43

"And don't they make you laugh? Have you ever gone by a field where their fuzzy yellow heads are waving without a care?"

"No," said Peter. "I've never really thought about dandelions being anything but an old weed you can't do anything with. You can't even pick them—they close up and turn ugly."

"Each to his own taste," said Grandma, "but *I* love them. Dandelions, rhubarb, and ladybugs on the windowsill—they all come together. They're the first signs of spring."

Peter jumped up and stamped his foot down on a black beetle making its way across the driveway.

Grandma Bagley shook her head. "So you've got it in for bugs, too? Now how would you like it if some giant saw you scurrying home with an armful of groceries and decided to step on you, just to hear you crunch? Suppose he didn't stop to wonder if you had a life of your own, going to school, playing ball, cutting my lawn. Suppose he thought of you as just a bug with no value."

Peter said nothing, but thought of the bird.

Grandma continued, "You know, everything has a value and a place. We are all part of God's creation, along with the stars and oceans and sunsets. We are all connected as a family—God's family—from a woolly bear to a wolf. And we humans are God's caretakers for the world. It's wonderful to be part of a big family like that. Everything grows according to its nature. Dandelions grow on lawns, whether we want them to or not. Cabbage worms eat cabbages, and birds eat worms, and cats eat birds, owls eat mice, and flies. . . ." Grandma sighed, "well, I am hard pressed to think what good flies are. Sometimes I think God must have made them on a bad day."

"Frogs eat flies," offered Peter, hopefully.

"I sure hope so. Well, enough talk. There's more work to do, and I must not hold you up. Besides, I have some dandelion heads to pick."

"What for?" asked Peter, curious. "You'll see," said Grandma, and snipped off forty dandelion heads into a paper bag.

For the rest of the afternoon, Peter looked about the world of Grandma Bagley's lawn with new eyes. He saw things he had not noticed before. He watched a mother bird nudging two fledglings off the wire to fly. They would not budge, despite her angry scolding and chattering. Finally, one took off followed by the other, shakily at first. Then they gained speed and courage, and they soared and dipped and made figure eights while their mother watched in pride.

He watched a tree squirrel swing from the chestnut tree to the elm, as gracefully as a trapeze artist. He watched a hummingbird hover in a whir of wings over a yellow rose and bees nuzzling the nectar of the horse chestnut blossoms.

The door to a new world had been opened, ever so slightly, to Peter today. He wished he knew why these creatures did these things. He wondered if they had families and chores and a time to be home for dinner. Did they ever play games? Maybe he would stop at the library sometime and find the answers.

Grandma called to him from the kitchen. "Peter, you've done enough work for today. Good job! Come on in."

Peter cleaned the grass off the blades and wheeled the lawn mower back into the shed until next week. He looked over the dandelionless carpet of green with its neat edges, and he was proud of his work. He guessed this was how a barber felt when he had just finished a haircut.

Grandma had a glass of milk and a piece of warm rhubarb pie waiting for him. The pie had a strangely golden crunchy top. But he ate it hungrily and pronounced it delicious. Grandma Bagley laughed, "I thought you said dandelions weren't good for anything. Would you believe there are petals from forty dandelion heads in that scrumptious crust?"

Peter said nothing. Then he asked quietly, suspiciously, "There aren't any ladybugs in it, are there?"

Grandma hugged him and said, "No, I couldn't find any."

Peter walked home slowly, five crisp dollar bills and the recipe for the pie in his pocket. The daisies and buttercups waved at him from either side of the road. They seemed to be waiting for a parade. He stopped and picked up a dead moth, still lovely and untouched. It was the delicate green of a lime, with long, fluttering tails. He cupped it in his hands carefully and walked faster. Perhaps he could get to the library before it closed.

Rhubarb Pie with Dandelion Topping

4 cups rhubarb, cut up
2 cups sugar
cinnamon & nutmeg
4 tablespoons flour
2 tablespoons butter

Put all of these into an unbaked pastry shell of your own recipe. Then make the topping.

Topping

Into a blender put the following:

½ cup cream (or half and half)
1 egg
2 tablespoons flour
the yellow petals of 40 dandelions

Run the blender for one minute and pour the topping on the pie. Sprinkle on cinnamon. Bake in a 350-degree oven for about 45 minutes, or until top is golden-flecked with brown from the cinnamon.

47

* 5 *

Rose-Annette and the Painted Lady

It had been a month since Rose-Annette and her family had moved from one small town in the northern tip of Maine to another small town where the people and weather and even the way of dressing were so very different.

In the beginning, she and her two sisters were excited about the move—having new rooms to explore, neighbors close by, a corner grocery store, being able to walk to school and church. They had lived far from everything in Maine, where their father had been a forest ranger. Now he had taken a job as a teacher in the Forestry Department of the college nearby, and her mother was happy that her family could share in the good things of this community life—piano lessons and Girl Scouts and sidewalks and movies!

Everyone *seemed* to be happy. Everyone but Rose-Annette, whose heart was filled with memories of her life in Aroostock. She missed her grandparents, *Pepere* and *Memere*, who lived over the border in New

Brunswick, Canada. At night, the tears came, and she sobbed as quietly as possible into the pillow which held all her secrets. "Why," she asked God, not angrily but sadly, "did things have to change? Why couldn't they stay the same forever?"

Some of the tears must have escaped her pillow, for her mother came in one night and quietly caressed Rose-Annette's long brown hair. She didn't ask what was wrong because she knew. She too had a sadness in her heart for leaving all she had ever known.

"Now, now, it's the way life is, little one," she said softly. "It's like one chapter ending and another brand new one beginning. Remember how I used to read you *The Wind in the Willows,* and each night you couldn't wait for the next chapter to find out what mischief Ratty or Toad had gotten into? So we've got to let the old chapters go, even though we hate to see them end. And we've got to have the faith that what lies ahead will be as happy as what is past. You understand?"

Rose-Annette shook her head yes, but sighed, "Why couldn't Daddy teach back in Maine? Why do just *we* have to change? Nobody else had to move."

"Now, you know that's not the way it is. Everything and everybody changes, whether we like it or not. Look at Marie, just toddling around. Before you know it, she will be a big girl like you, and you won't even remember how she looked when she was two. And someday *you'll* be talking to *your* little girl like this—oh dear," Rose-Annette's mother began sniffling. "Aren't we a good pair, crying over such silly things!"

And they both laughed and hugged, and Rose-Annette went to sleep resolving that she would try to look for all the good things in this new chapter of her life, starting tomorrow.

For one thing, she liked her new school and friends. She had been nervous that first day, walking into the classroom filled with unfamiliar faces. Mrs. Bunwether, her teacher, asked her to come up to her desk and tell her classmates about herself, and she did. After that, Maggie came up to her shyly and said, "I like the way you talk, your words run together like a stream, all up and down and bubbly." Rose-Annette beamed. She had been afraid they would make fun of her accent when she spoke English.

"Yes," said Mrs. Bunwether, "Rose-Annette's grandparents are French, and her family is what we call Franco-American. . . ."

Anthony began to snicker. He caught Peter's eye, and then Timothy's, and the three of them began to laugh out loud. Mrs. Bunwether was not laughing.

"What is so funny, Anthony?" she asked coldly,

fixing her eye upon him as if to pin him in his seat.

"She sounds like a can of spaghetti!" And then everyone, including Rose-Annette, began to laugh. Anthony, now the center of attention, jumped up and said loudly, "And I LOVE Franco-American spaghetti!"

After that, Rose-Annette felt at home; and each day more and more of her loneliness faded away. Her new friends introduced her to Grandma Bagley, who welcomed her with a *"Bonjour,* Rose-Annette!" and a hug.

"You know," she said, "once when I was in Nova Scotia, I had a most delicious pork pie—"

"Tourtière!" said Rose-Annette joyfully.

"That's it! Would your mother have the recipe?"

"Oh, yes, I'll bring it next time I come."

"Good. And in return, I shall give you a bouquet of flowers for her. Come along."

As Grandma filled her basket with poppies, Rose-Annette saw a black caterpillar on a hollyhock leaf. It had white spots and yellow side markings. "Ugh," she stared at it, "what an ugly thing!"

"True," agreed Grandma, "but the loveliest of butterflies may come from such an ugly creature, so let's not hurt its feelings! This one seems fully grown, almost ready to turn into its chrysalis."

"Its what?"

"Chrysalis—it comes from a Greek word meaning gold. It's like a nutshell, which the caterpillar spins around itself—a house to grow in. It will hang from a stem or twig, or even a jar lid—let's go see if we can find one." They went into the house, carrying the treasure carefully. Soon the caterpillar on its hollyhock stem stood upright in a clean mayonnaise jar, with the jar lid screwed on loosely and holes punched in the top.

"Now you put in a few hollyhock leaves fresh daily and watch. Before you know it, the caterpillar will spin its house, and you will have a chrysalis hanging from the jar lid."

"And then what?"

"Then you wait for the butterfly. That nutshell it weaves will split right down the back and there it is," Grandma said. "It won't look much like a butterfly at first, all limp and wet and stuck-together. But soon it starts pumping the fluid from its body into the veins of its wings until they smooth out from the body and become straight. Sort of like pumping up your bicycle wheels when they're flat. Then it waves them up and down to dry, and then it just takes off and flies away, like a beautiful gypsy."

Rose-Annette held the jar tenderly to her. "Oh, I wonder what kind it is—blue or purple or yellow with red dots—"

"I'll look it up and tell you. Right away. Tonight," Peter said, feeling very important. "I'll go to the library and check out what kind of butterflies come from ugly black caterpillars with white spots and hairy prickles."

True to his word, Peter showed up at Rose-Annette's house after supper, impatient for the honor of bearing his important information. He cleared his throat. "What you've got, Rose-Annette, is a Thistle Butterfly, or Painted Lady, who lays her eggs and lives on thistles, hollyhocks, and marsh mallows."

"Marshmallows?" laughed Cecile, Rose-Annette's sister.

"No. *Marsh* mallows. Pink flowers that grow in marshes."

"A Thistle Butterfly! Oh, that's lovely. I've always loved thistles." added Rose-Annette.

"The Painted Lady," Peter continued, "belongs to the Vanessa or Angel-Wings tribe . . ."

"Vanessa—oh, that's elegant! I think that's what I'll call her. Vanessa, the Painted Lady. She's *got* to be beautiful with that name."

"The Painted Lady," Peter read on determinedly, "is one of the most adventurous of butterflies. She is a hardy traveler, crossing long distances and oceans to get where she wants to be. She has traveled from Africa to Europe and has been found in Labrador and among the flowering pink almond blossoms in Sicily in spring.

"And listen to this—sometimes in a snowy woods during a midwinter thaw, you can find them flitting about as if it were summer. And, listen to *this,* one explorer said that he had climbed Mt. Hood, '11,000 feet into Heaven,' and there at the peak he found Painted Ladies hovering and waiting for the wind to catch them and whirl them about as joyfully as children take their sleds in a snowstorm and go down the steepest hills."

"Can you *imagine*," said Rose-Annette, in a whisper, "butterflies in winter! And here's Vanessa, right here on the dining room table! How much longer must we wait?"

"It says," said Peter, flipping the pages, "that in a

few days the chrysalis will be formed and then about ten more days." Annette wondered how she could ever wait that long.

Before she knew it, it had happened. The caterpillar was gone. She had disappeared into the home she had spun. Each morning, Rose-Annette woke to see if Vanessa had performed her magic act and popped out from her golden shell. And, on the eleventh day, she had.

She could not have been long in the world, for she sat crumpled, limp, shivering, on the edge of the jar. She began to pump and wave and straighten her wings, just as Grandma described, until finally she was truly a butterfly, truly a Painted Lady.

Rose-Annette had never seen anything quite so beautiful and she wondered how much time it must have taken God to figure out the design and colors of this creation. There were so many shades of red and brown and gray and rose and lemon, white patches, peacock eyespots, all mingled and marbled together on her four wings, which had lacy edges, as if her petticoat were showing.

Before she could call her family to come see the miracle, the butterfly, her wings now dry, lifted off unsteadily from the jar, and flew directly for the open window, eager for her very first taste of wildflower nectar.

"Oh, Vanessa, come back, please," Rose-Annette cried, "I've only known you a few moments!" She ran to the window, but the butterfly was gone. She knew in her heart that she would not see her again. Vanessa was, after all, born to be a traveler. Rose-Annette won-

dered where the Painted Lady would fly first. Would she soar above the seas to sip almond tea in Sicily, on her way to summer among Alpine thistles and eidelweiss? Would she fly fearlessly into snowy winds?

She wondered if Vanessa would ever remember her days as an ugly black caterpillar. She seemed to have left that life behind her along with her shell. Rose-Annette wondered if, when the time came, she would fly out into the unknown with as much joy as Vanessa had. Where would Rose-Annette travel with the wind, and what lovely design would God have painted on her? Perhaps she would be an explorer or mountain-climber or astronaut or butterfly-photographer or basketball coach. Perhaps she would be all of them.

She knew that anything is possible when you begin a new chapter.

* 6 *

Timothy's Special Day

Today was the day for which Timothy had waited these many months—for one year, to be exact. Ever since the grand closing outburst of fireworks at last year's Fire Department Picnic, Timothy had counted the days until it would happen again, and now that marvelous day was here! When the sun came through his window and woke him that morning, he bounced up and threw his arms out as if to hug God.

Timothy reached under the bed and pulled out the pickle jar that held the nickels and pennies and dimes he had saved and counted them once more. He had $15.46. He dreamed again of how he would spend it: barbecued chicken, chili dogs, corn roasted in the husks, lemonade with slices of real lemon in it, double dip ice-cream cones covered with chocolate and sprinkled with peanuts. He licked his lips at the thought. And the rides—the Octopus and the Dodge 'Em cars and, of course, the roller coaster.

He and Anthony always went on the roller coaster together. Separately, they were terrified; together, they were just medium-scared. Anthony said that this year the first one who screamed had to pay for the next ride, and Timothy said for sure it wouldn't be *him*. Anthony's family was to pick Timothy up after lunch, just in time for the Tug-of-War contest and the Performing Poodles Circus Act. Timothy's family was going to his grandmother's farm for a picnic. Timothy wished he could be in both places at the same time, but Timothy's mother understood and said his grandmother would, too. There would be other picnics this summer. So Timothy happily helped load the car with baskets of food and jugs of raspberry iced tea and folding chairs and badminton racquets. He waved goodbye to them, feeling just a little bit sad that he wasn't with them.

But not for long. He sat on the front porch steps and imagined how it would be to hear the parade beginning, with the long, slow wail of the fire siren warning one and all to make clear the way for the marching bands! He could see the red-and-white uniforms marching sharp and stiff as wooden soldiers, and he could hear the cymbals clashing, the drums throbbing and deafening him as they passed by, the glittering tinkle of the glockenspiel. Oh, would Anthony never come!

He counted all the red cars that went by. He bounced a ball against the side of the house where there were no windows. He went to the garden and found three green beans, which he ate, and a small prickly cucumber, which he didn't. He dialed Anthony's number, but no one answered. He went back to the porch and watched the clock inch its way to 4 P.M.

He looked at the *National Geographic* magazine, but even the pictures of monstrous sharks could not hold his interest. Then, at 5 P.M., he heard the real siren, faint, then stronger, followed by oompahs of the tubas and the muffled thunder of the drums.

Timothy leaned against the screen door and cried, quietly at first and then in big, choking gulps. This was his special day, and now it was going on without him, as if he didn't matter. He was stuck here by himself, no rides, no food, no fireworks—oh, the fireworks! Not just firecrackers and sparklers but *real* fireworks, rockets and showers of sparks and bursting cannons— and he would miss them all. Why did he depend on Anthony? What kind of a friend was Anthony?

Timothy's stomach began to growl. When he opened the refrigerator he saw that all the good things had gone to his grandmother's. He found a few slices of bologna and rolled them onto a piece of white bread spread thickly with mustard. He pretended it was a hot dog and went back to the front steps to eat it. It was turning twilight when he saw a familiar figure with white hair bobbing down the sidewalk. It was Grandma Bagley with a small basket hanging from her arm. He wiped away his tears and waved. She waved back and continued walking past. Then she stopped, turned around, and came back to his front steps.

"Why, Timothy, I thought you and Anthony were going to make a day of it at the Fireman's Picnic."

"We were, but he went on without me. He never called or anything." Timothy's eyes began to blink again.

"Now, Timothy," said Grandma gently, "don't go jumping to conclusions. He must have a very good explanation. He might even have gotten sick."

"Then why didn't he call me?" asked Timothy, unconvinced.

"Well, you've got to give him a chance to explain. It's like counting to ten before you get angry. Friends have to trust each other, don't they? In the meantime," she opened her basket, "would you mind sharing some of my goodies with me? I've been working at the church social all day, and they asked me to take these leftovers. I couldn't possibly eat them all."

Timothy perked up at the good smells coming out of the basket. He looked in and saw hot baked beans, crispy chicken wings, deviled eggs, watermelon pickle, and half a blueberry pie. "Oh boy, does that look good," he sighed. "I'm *so* hungry!"

They went into the kitchen and got paper plates, silverware, and a red-checked tablecloth. Soon the feast was spread out on the picnic table on the front porch.

"Timothy, I'm so glad I didn't have to eat all this by myself. This is a real celebration!" They ate and talked until Timothy licked the last blueberry off his plate and the dark red sky turned to purple and finally black. Slowly, here and there, as if by signal, tiny lights blinked in the sky. Timothy saw them first in the spice bush and then in the large fir tree which his father strung with lights at Christmas. Finally they were all around him, merrily sparking the sky.

Timothy's eyes grew large. "Oh, wow, Grandma, look at them! I've never seen so many fireflies in my life!"

Grandma Bagley marveled with Timothy at what seemed to be a convention of all the fireflies in the world. "Aren't they incredible?" she said. "It's as if God switched these fireworks on and they won't stop! When I was very little, I used to watch them through the window when I went to bed. I thought they were fairies dancing at a Midsummer's Eve Ball, putting on a performance just for me. Once they lined up on a clothesline like a string of diamonds. And once, my parents put a record on the Victrola downstairs and it seemed as if the fireflies were tiny ballerinas, dipping and swaying."

"Wow, look at all of them," Timothy repeated, as if

he hadn't heard a word Grandma said. A few fireflies came close to his shoelaces. "Will they bite?" he asked.

"Oh, no," Grandma whispered. "They're friend, not foe. You know, there's a place in South America where they blink red and green, and people use them as lanterns to find their way out of the forests."

"Wow, look at all of them," said Timothy, as he watched them hover about his feet. Then they heard a sound, a small one but one which would not be ignored, a single, forlorn *galump.* It sounded like the twanging of a loose cello string. Gradually, it was joined by other *galumpings,* to which were added *harrumps, kerplunks,* and *brrriggits.* The sounds grew loud and took over their ears, just as the fireflies had hypnotized their eyes.

"Timothy, I think we have a concert beginning!"

"Frogs! Sounds like hundreds. Thousands."

"I'd say at *least* fifty. What a noisy bunch—I think they need a good conductor to straighten them out!"

Timothy could not imagine a funnier chorus. It seemed that each frog had its own special tune and cared not the least what the next one was singing. There were grandpa croakers, who sang one single precise bass note, and high-pitched nervous tenors, who sang *brrriggitty* songs without stopping. Then there were those who sounded as if they had just gulped down an oyster, whole.

The blinking fireflies punctuated the frogs' music. Timothy and Grandma were laughing so hard that they almost didn't notice Anthony and his family pulling up in their car. Anthony, slinking in his seat, looked downcast. His father opened the door and said,

"Anthony, I think you have something to say to Timothy."

Anthony walked slowly up to Timothy, and everyone in the car was silent.

"I'm sorry, Timothy. It's all my fault you didn't go. The car wouldn't start this morning, and we didn't think we'd get to go. I was supposed to call you and tell you before your folks left. But I forgot. And then when my Dad got the truck going, we had to jump in quick because he couldn't shut the motor off, and I forgot all about you. Until I got to the roller coaster and then it was too late. I'm really sorry, honest."

"So, who did you go on the roller coaster with?"

"No one. I went by myself. Boy, was it awful! I'll never do that again. It's not so scary when you're with me. I even threw up my root beer."

Timothy smiled. Grandma was right. You had to wait and listen before you got angry. Still, he wasn't *really* sorry about the root beer.

Timothy's family soon followed Anthony's into the driveway. Now there were almost as many people as fireflies, most of them tired, cranky, and sunburned. Timothy's sister was crying because some of her toasted marshmallow was stuck in her hair. Anthony's mother brought out the double fudge chocolate cake she had won at a raffle. Grandma Bagley reached into her basket, pulled out a sparkler, stuck it in the center of the cake, and lit it.

The children screamed with delight as the sparks shot up into the air, and even the weary parents smiled. "What a lovely ending to a lovely day," said

Timothy's mother, pulling the last tangle of marshmallow out of her daughter's hair.

Timothy looked at Grandma Bagley. Nobody else seemed to notice the fireflies and the frogs. She smiled back. It was their secret. The awful day had turned out to be a special day, one which he would always remember, even when he grew older and no longer rode roller coasters.

* 7 *

Strazzlecherrygoosel-currantblackandbluebarb Marmalade (with two green apples)

When Anthony and his mother stepped into Grandma Bagley's kitchen that August morning and found her stirring the sputtering pot of her famous Apricot-Pineapple-Peach Conserve, Anthony knew that the time had come. The kitchen was bursting with the sweet golden smell of the cooking fruit, and it made Anthony all the more impatient to be on his way. His mother had brought Grandma special jelly jars from the store, the kind with round bottoms and screw-on caps with flowers painted on them.

Grandma thanked them, explaining, "You need special jars for a special jam, especially when it is going to be entered in the fair," as she patted her forehead dry. She always came home with at least one first prize ribbon.

"Can't stop to visit, Grandma, I have jamming of my own to do!" Anthony said. His mother waved good-bye, and they were on their way. Grandma didn't mind at all, because, whenever she had to talk and make jam at the same time, the jam burnt. She did wonder what was wrong with Anthony.

She didn't know that Anthony had a very special dream. He didn't want to ride in the milk truck and help Joe deliver milk, or to catch a mackerel as fat as any his father brought home, or to sit on his neighbor's motorcycle and pretend he was riding it over sand dunes in the desert.

No, Anthony wanted to make a batch of jam, right from scratch, all by himself. He had longed to do this since last summer, when he and his mother had gone to the country to search the woods and bogs and abandoned orchards for fruit. They made a day of it, leaving after the dishes had been washed and Anthony had made his bed so there were no lumps in it.

They searched out wild strawberries, low-lying dewberries, or the gleanings left by the blueberry rakers. He wore an old flannel shirt, buttoned at the wrists, so the thorns would not tear his skin. Still, prickly vines clung to him, like the boney fingers of a witch who would not turn him loose.

Anthony helped by getting into all the nooks and crannies his mother couldn't reach. He climbed the crabapple tree and shook the rosy nuggets free. He squished about the banks of streams and picked elderberries. He cut the ends from gooseberries with his own knife.

When they got home, he helped hull the berries

and pick off stems and leaves. He measured sugar
without spilling it and put wax in the old metal teapot
to melt. It was exciting to watch his mother fill the
jars. The jelly sparkled like rubies.

But now he was a year older. He did not want help.
He wanted to do it all by himself. He dreamed of bring-
ing out a jar of his very own Red Currant Jelly on a
cold December morning to spread on his English
muffin. He dreamed of entering his jam at the Blue
Hill Fair, standing right alongside Grandma Bagley
with her marvelous conserve, and being awarded first
prize for the most wonderful jam in the fair, in the
United States, maybe even Canada. He thought how

sad Grandma would feel to lose. Maybe he would refuse the ribbon and graciously turn it over to her. Maybe he wouldn't. He hadn't decided yet.

But he kept his dream to himself for fear he might be laughed at if he told. First, he would gather the fruit, and then he would tell his plan.

Anthony discovered this was easier said than done. He could not find enough of any one fruit to make even one jar of jam. He started out with high hopes and an empty pail, sniffing for the sweet piney smell of raspberries. He could find none. And when he found the currant and gooseberry bushes, the birds had already been there for breakfast. He climbed the hill only to find that the blueberries were still hard and pink, and the cranberries were still green.

Anthony was depressed. He had gone to all the places he and his mother had picked last year. Where else could he look?

Anthony moped. Anthony sulked. And he would not tell his mother what was wrong. He pushed aside his peanut butter and honey sandwich and kicked the table leg over and over. His mother's patience grew thin, and she suggested that he make himself useful instead of spreading gloom.

She said, "Anthony, please go out to the garden and pick some peas, beans, one onion, three carrots, a zucchini, and a sprig of dill. We will have them as mixed vegetables tonight. How do you think that will taste?"

Anthony didn't answer. He just made a face and did what he was told. He didn't *care* how they would taste; they were only vegetables. But as he picked and thought, a wonderful idea began to spark and pop about inside his head.

He brought the vegetables to his mother, smiling and almost jumping with excitement. "Well," she said, giving him a funny look. "I never knew work to cause such an instant cure. *Anthony,* stop hopping or my cake will fall—you must have fleas!" She rushed to the oven to rescue the cake.

Anthony was quite happy now. The next morning, he got up, ate a bowlful of cornflakes with a banana, washed his bowl, and put on his old flannel shirt. He tied a lard pail to his belt and was off to the fields before anyone else was up. His mission was to pick whatever fruit he found, on whichever path he followed, wherever it led.

He followed the flight of a purple butterfly and stopped by a Juneberry tree. He found six berries, all in one cluster. Into his pail they went. Beneath the tree were several bushes, and Anthony's eye caught the crimson of currants. Another bush hung heavy with green gooseberries. They joined the Juneberries, and the bottom of the pail was covered.

Anthony picked his way through the grass, which was still heavy with dew, and found a patch of glistening black dewberries. They were not as large as thimbleberries, but their taste was as sweet. He crossed to a field where he remembered seeing blueberry blossoms in the spring, and—sure enough—there they were, fat and ripe and covered with a velvet blue blush. With them, the pail was one-third full.

He hurried from the field to the path that led to the shore. Hanging from the craggy ledges were

chokecherries in heavy abundance. He jumped up to catch the branches with one hand and picked a few with the other.

Anthony climbed over the wreck of a wooden boat that had washed ashore before he was born, and up the rocks where the raspberry canes sparkled with the red fruit in the sun. They reminded Anthony of the candy raspberries he found in his Christmas stocking. The sun had dried the dew, and he began to feel hot and thirsty. His flannel shirt was sticking to him, and his sneakers were wet and the laces had come untied.

Before he had a chance to tie them, Anthony tripped and stumbled over a woodchuck hole. But he held tightly to his precious pail, and not a berry spilled! Anthony's heart thumped and he could feel it pounding in his ears and throat. Where he had fallen, he saw the leaf of the wild strawberry. By some miracle—it was long past the time for strawberries—there were a handful of late stragglers, cone-shaped beauties, calmly waiting for Anthony to come along and plop them into his pail. Which he did.

A chipmunk chattered at him from an apple tree, and as Anthony looked up at it, two small, gnarled green apples fell at his feet. *Well,* he thought, as he picked them up, *if they want to get into the jam, too, why not?*

Anthony started home. He had just reached the kitchen door when he noticed one red stalk of rhubarb that had not yet gone to seed. It looked lonely in the small garden under the window, so he picked it and laid it atop the pail mounded high with fruit.

Anthony's neck had little red bumps of mosquito

bites and his arms were scratched from the thorns. His feet squished as he walked. He felt proud as he showed the fruit to his mother and told her what he would like to do. She stood there, wiping her hands on her apron, looking surprised and pleased.

"I think that's a great idea, Anthony. Let's do it!" She got eight small jars that had once held mustard and honey and candied cherries. Anthony got out the jam pot and sugar and teapot for melting the wax. He spread the fruit on a paper towel and examined his treasures as if they were jewels.

He pitted the cherries and stemmed the currants, then cut the rhubarb and green apples into small pieces. He pulled blueberry leaves and a little white spider out of the rest of the fruit. Then he crushed it all together with the potato masher in the jam pot and watched the juices and colors run together. But he needed something else.

He looked around. In the center of the table was an English Marmalade crock filled with nasturtiums. That was it! He would make a marmalade instead of a plain jam. In the refrigerator he found half a lemon and a small orange on its way to becoming dried up. He sliced these very thin, as thin as he could without slicing his fingers, and added them to the pot.

His mother lit the stove, and slowly, carefully, he stirred the fruit and added the sugar. Soon the fruit began to sputter up in thick bubbles that broke like blisters. The color turned from crimson to purple and foamed up pink, and the kitchen was filled with the perfume of the fruit of the fields.

Anthony's mother tested the jam as it dripped

from the spoon and pronounced it ready. As she filled each jar, Anthony stuck a knife inside each one so the glass wouldn't crack from the heat. Soon the jars were full. Anthony poured the hot wax from the teapot into each jar to keep them sealed forever. His dream had become real!

He spread some of the hot skimmings on a corn muffin and sat down by himself on the back steps. Never had he tasted anything so good in his life. And he had done it all himself, with just a little help from his mother.

When he came in to get another muffin, his mother asked, "Anthony, what will you call your jam?" Anthony thought a long time. He took out a pencil and filled a sheet of paper with words and scratchings-out. Finally he looked up with a great smile and said, "I've

got it! I've got just the right name—" And he read
slowly,

"*Strazzlecherrygooselcurrantblackandbluebarb
Marmalade.*"

"Oh my," said his mother, looking very serious.
"How will that ever fit on the label?"

"With," Anthony continued reading, "two green
apples."